FRIGHT SCHOOL

Janet Lawler

pictures by Chiara Galletti

Albert Whitman & Company
Chicago, Illinois

To Jackson, Mitchell, Perry, and Grace—JL
To "child Chiara"—CG

Library of Congress Cataloging-in-Publication Data

Names: Lawler, Janet, author. | Galletti, Chiara, illustrator.
Title: Fright School / Janet Lawler; pictures by Chiara Galletti.
Description: Chicago, Illinois: Albert Whitman and Company, 2018.
Summary: "Little monsters head to Fright School to learn the art
of scaring trick-or-treaters"—Provided by publisher.
Identifiers: LCCN 2017057984 | ISBN 9780807525531 (hardcover)
Subjects: | CYAC: Stories in rhyme. | Monsters—Fiction. |
Schools—Fiction. | Halloween—Fiction. | Fear—Fiction.
Classification: LCC PZ8.3.L355 Fri 2018 | DDC [E]—dc23
LC record available at https://lccn.loc.gov/2017057984

Printed in China
10 9 8 7 6 5 4 3 2 1 WKT 22 21 20 19 18

Design by Rick DeMonico

For more information about Albert Whitman & Company,
visit our website at www.albertwhitman.com.

A darkened school on autumn nights,
with moonlight streaming in,
echoes with a midnight bell
for classes to begin.

The door to Fright School opens wide.

Each monster grabs a seat
to learn the art of scaring
all the kids who trick-or-treat.

WELCOME!

Mummies practice moaning sounds
and dragging just one foot.

Draculas in coffins rise.
Their teacher scolds,

"Stay put!"

Goblins leer in mirrors,
earning As for every scare.

Werewolves in the older grades
are taught to spike their hair.

Bats hang out in gloomy rooms
or swoop across the halls.

Ghosts appear and disappear
while seeping through the walls.

At lunchtime picky eaters groan,

"Our apples don't taste rotten!"

Witches relish hotdogs
made last year and then forgotten.

And then at Fright School recess,
zombies wander in a daze.

Spiders on the jungle gym
create a playground maze.

The janitor tells birds of prey
to wipe their dirty claws.

The nurse yells from her office,
"Hey, I'm running out of gauze!"

Vampires sharpen up their grins
by filing teeth to points.

Skeletons bone up on math,
subtracting ribs from joints.

Trolls burst out of lockers,
swinging fists and smelling foul.

Ghouls play in the music room,
perfecting hoots and howls.

Weeks later, when the term is done,
each creature takes a test.

Awards are won for boiling brews
and haunting houses best.

They clutch their new diplomas
just in time for Halloween.

Tossing hats and hugging cats, all cheer,

"Let's make a scene!"

Suddenly they hear a noise,
a muffled, heavy thump,
followed by a forceful knock.
In unison, they jump.

"Who's that?" the biggest bat squeaks out,
as fearful monsters quake.
At last, one goblin grabs the knob
and gives a nervous shake.

Fright School students crack the door
and peer out toward the street.

But lessons get forgotten...

when the kids cry,
"TRICK or TREAT!"